LOVE IS...

... A GENTLE PAIR OF HANDS

... THAT FEELING THAT MAKES YOUR HEART BEAT FASTER

... FORGETTING HOW GOOD MAMA'S COOKING WAS

... PAINTING EASTER EGGS TOGETHER

and the tender feeling that makes you want to tell what LOVE IS ... to that very special someone in your life.

Other SIGNETTES You Will Enjoy

- ☐ **MORE LOVE IS by Kim Grove.** (#T6199—75¢)
- ☐ **LOVE IS #3 by Kim Grove.** (#T6200—75¢)
- ☐ **LOVE IS #4 by Kim Grove.** (#T6201—75¢)
- ☐ **LOVE IS #5 by Kim Grove.** (#T6202—75¢)
- ☐ **LOVE IS #6 by Kim Grove.** (#T6203—75¢)
- ☐ **LOVE IS #7 by Kim Grove.** (#T6126—75¢)
- ☐ **LOVE IS #8 by Kim Grove.** (#T5938—75¢)
- ☐ **HOW TO CROCHET by Janice Harrison.** (#P5647—60¢)
- ☐ **NEEDLEPOINT by Janice Harrison.** (#P5184—60¢)
- ☐ **1974 CALORIE GUIDE TO BRAND NAMES & BASIC FOODS by Barbara Kraus.** (#Q5893—95¢)
- ☐ **1974 CARBOHYDRATE GUIDE TO BRAND NAMES & BASIC FOODS by Barbara Kraus.** (#Q5894—95¢)

THE NEW AMERICAN LIBRARY, INC.,
P.O. Box 999, Bergenfield, New Jersey 07621

Please send me the SIGNETTE BOOKS I have checked above. I am enclosing $______________(check or money order—no currency or C.O.D.'s). Please include the list price plus 25¢ a copy to cover handling and mailing costs. (Prices and numbers are subject to change without notice.)

Name______________________________

Address____________________________

City______________State__________Zip Code________

Allow at least 3 weeks for delivery

LOVE IS . . . #9

by
Kim Grove

A SIGNET BOOK
NEW AMERICAN LIBRARY
TIMES MIRROR

For Malaika

Copyright © 1972, 1974 by Los Angeles Times Syndicate
All rights reserved

SIGNET TRADEMARK REG. U.S. PAT. OFF. AND FOREIGN COUNTRIES
REGISTERED TRADEMARK—MARCA REGISTRADA
HECHO EN CHICAGO, U.S.A.

SIGNET, SIGNET CLASSICS, MENTOR, PLUME
and MERIDIAN BOOKS
are published by The New American Library, Inc.,
1301 Avenue of the Americas, New York, New York 10019.

First Printing, September, 1974

3 4 5 6 7 8 9

PRINTED IN THE UNITED STATES OF AMERICA

...calling him at the office and playing "Eternally" to him.

love is . . .
. . . a gentle pair of arms.

love is ...

... letting him light his pipe at the table after dinner.

love is ...

. . . *forgiving an overdrawn bank account.*

. . . letting her sleep a little longer.

love is ...

. . . studying together for exams.

love is ...
. . . keeping the peace as much as possible.

love is ...

. . . calling her frequently when you are out of town.

love is...

...being able to say you're sorry.

love is...

. . . painting the rooms her favorite color.

...helping her with the dishes at mid-night after a big dinner party.

. . . forgetting the Joans, Jeans and might-have-beens.

. . . saying it with roses on Valentine's Day.

love is . . .

. . . having matching outfits.

love is ...
YOU
US
ME
Kim
. . . compromising when you have conflicting opinions.

love is ...

. . . *choosing the photo which is most flattering to her.*

. . . gently squeezing her hand.

love is ...

. . . cheering her up when she feels sad.

... getting the Tom Jones fever just to please her.

love is . . .

. . . being understanding when he gets mad.

love is ...

. . . being there whenever he needs you.

love is...
Kim
. . . thinking about him when you first wake up.

love is...
. . . telling each other with your eyes.

love is ...

. . . that feeling which makes your heart beat faster.

love is ...

. . . turning down the radio when she has a headache.

...opening the door before he gets his key in the lock.

love is...
. . . turning up the heat before she gets out of bed.

love is ...

. . . the big smile you wear when she tells you she's going to be a mother.

love is...

. . . treating her tenderly when she's suffering from morning sickness.

love is ...
kim
. . . helping your
working wife with
the chores.

love is ...

. . . not mentioning his thinning hair.

love is...

. . . trying to keep the telephone bill low.

love is ...

. . . giving in, not giving up.

love is...
9
kim
. . . feeling like you're on cloud nine.

love is...

. . . believing that when he kisses the hurt it will go away.

. . . when you promise to return and do.

love is ...
Kim
. . . listening to her woes.

love is...
Kim
...letting her keep
the big, hairy dog.

love is . . .

. . . making up quickly after a row.

love is...
... enjoying your-
self now—it's later
than you think.

. . . not being possessive.

love is ...

. . . not mentioning the wrinkles under her eyes.

love is ...

. . . helping her dry those tears when she's upset.

. . . bringing her some flowers on a rainy day.

. . . letting her choose the color of the new car.

... when you avoid criticizing his relatives.

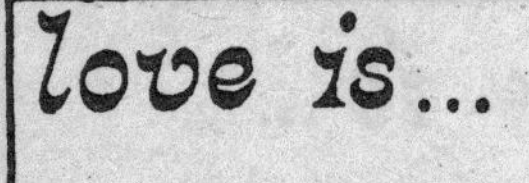

. . . seeing she gets plenty of rest as an expectant mother.

. . . not betraying her trust.

. . . meaning every kiss.

love is . . .

. . . being able to say what's on your mind.

love is...

... forgetting how good mama's cooking was.

love is ...
Kim
...letting her watch her favorite TV program.

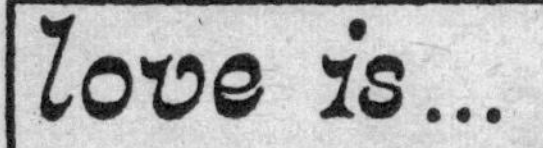

. . . painting Easter eggs together.

. . . not calling her on April Fool's Day pretending to be Engelbert Humperdinck.

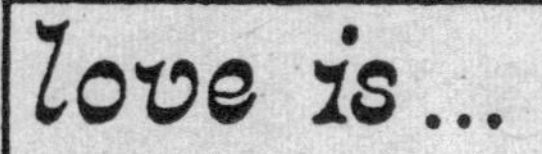

. . . supervising her exercise program.

. . . going out for a pizza when she's too tired to cook.

. . . admiring her new dress.

love is...

. . . making something for him instead of watching TV.

love is...

. . . trying to over-look some of his faults.

love is...
...clearing the coffee table after him several times a day.

love is ...

. . . answering her nasty words with kind words.

love is...

. . . his smile as he comes home from his trip.

love is...
. . . keeping quiet while he's studying.

love is...

...knowing you're always number one with him.

love is...

. . . dancing cheek to cheek.

love is...

...helping her wax the furniture.

. . . making him a box lunch.

. . . backing up his fish stories.

love is...

. . . trying not to be angry at the same time.

love is...

. . . the funny feeling you get the first time he tells you.

love is...
... pretending you don't know what time he came home.
Kim

love is...
. . . believing he believes you when you're pretty sure he doesn't.

. . . getting front seats for Tom Jones' performance.

love is ...

. . . being together in joy and in sorrow.

love is...

. . . carrying her books for her.

love is . . .

. . . not dropping your ashes on the floor.

love is...

...having a chat in the evening instead of watching TV.

love is . . .

. . . not mentioning her first gray hair.

love is ...

. . . not telling his deepest secret.

. . . giving and for-giving.

love is . . .

. . . getting up first and making her morning coffee.

love is ...
Kim
. . . walking together under a bubble umbrella.

love is...
...when he prefers you to his car.

love is...
. . . reminiscing about your childhoods.

love is . . .

. . . not getting to eat all your lunch.

love is...
kim
. . . taking care of
yourself for her.

love is...

. . . keeping your fights short and few.

love is...
Kim
. . . picking out cloud shapes.

love is...
...cleaning up your old mess before making a new mess.

. . . giving her a rest from her chores on Mother's Day.

love is ...

. . . being able to admit it when you're wrong.

love is...
kim
. . . inviting her to
meet you for lunch.